# SPIRIT OF THE WHITE BISON

## Beatrice Culleton

### Illustrations by

## Robert Kakaygeesick Jr.

**Book Publishing Company**
**Summertown, Tennessee**

Originally published in Canada by Pemmican Publications, Inc:

Pemmican Publications, Inc., gratefully acknowledges the assistance accorded to its publishing program by the Manitoba Arts Council and the Canada Council.

Printed in the USA.

ISBN 0-913990-64-7                    LCCC# 89-32047

Library of Congress CIP data is available.

**Book Publishing Company**
**PO Box 99**
**Summertown, TN 38483**

# INTRODUCTION

When I originally set out to write this book, I had no strong feelings for bison. I knew they had provided life to the Indian people and later to the Metis people. I understood that the white buffalo, in particular, has special spiritual significance to the traditional Indian. This story is not one of their legends. With great respect to the elders, I simply wanted to write a Native story which might be suitable for animation.

In this story, a White Bison tells about the decimation of the buffalo. It was not a quiet, accidental extermination. The horror was that the killings were deliberate, planned, military actions. Destroy the livelihood of the Indians and win a war. 'Buffalo hunters' were heroes of that era, and lived on as legendary heroes of the American West. Was the war really won?

Worse, we do not worry about the decimation of the buffalo or the Indian people, anymore. Today, we have progressed to the position of worrying about the decimation of all mankind. Are we that ignorant that we haven't learned from past mistakes? Or do we pretend those mistakes didn't happen, shove them away in the past, and forget about them? It is true that our mistakes should be forgiven but only if we intend not to make those mistakes again. And how much can mistakes of magnitude be forgiven? Can we forgive the horrendous killings of six million people? And the last question is will there be anybody around to forgive a mistake that involves nuclear arms?

One of the most romanticized movies recently has been *Star Wars*. The *nuclear* word is in the news everyday, now. I used to think my future was bleak, not because I was Native, but because of the nuclear threat. I hope the adults of the future, even though you don't have the power of the vote today, will not let leaders allow a nuclear weapon to have the last word.

Having written about the direction of thought in which this story forced me, the thought of advanced technology in weapons (one of the most profitable businesses supported by taxpayers), I will say what I started out to say. I want to thank people like Myrt and Bill of Miami, Manitoba, for giving more meaning to this book. I want to say to those who had read or knew about this story, that I appreciate our talks.

Thank you to those with courage, vision and wisdom, who say no to nuclear arms, and to those leaders of other countries who say no to the leaders of the superpowers. I wanted to ask the anti-abortionists, the pro-lifers, what are you doing about the future of *your* children? Do you think about the nuclear arms race? And finally, I think it's ironic that one has to 'fight' for peace.

Beatrice Culleton

**Dedicated to**
**My daugther, my son and my husband.**
**— Bea**

# CHAPTER 1

Mama told me I was born on a warm spring day. It was in late afternoon after a brief shower and I was born under a rainbow. Mama said that made me special. I didn't feel special when I was young. I only felt very different. My name was the reason. I was called Little White Buffalo. And it was, of course, because my coat was white, unlike all the other buffalo, whose coats ranged from tan to dark brown.

The other youngsters in my group refused to let me play with them and the only time they paid attention to me was when they teased me and pushed me around. But I found other playmates like the birds and the prairie dogs and I did enjoy the games we played.

Most days I spent suckling milk and pretending I was nibbling at the prairie grasses. Mama would tell me which plants not to eat. It was very important to pay

strict attention to whatever we were taught. It could be
that we wouldn't have a second try at the lessons. I
could run as fast as the older bulls and cows and faster
than most of the younger buffalo. I had to because
sometimes they all chased me and I had to outrun them.
In our herd, there were millions of other buffalo, I
reckoned. Sometimes I would get lost among a strange
group and I'd have to yell my loudest for Mama to come
and find me. Great Bison, the bull who had sired me
and my many half-brothers and half-sisters, was the
largest, strongest bull in our group and it was natural
for him to be our group leader. While the older ones
made sure I was well looked-after, they didn't bother
protecting me from the other youngsters. I guess they
thought we ought to settle our differences between us.
The problem for me was that I was one against many.
Of course, if I had stayed by my mother's side, they
wouldn't have bothered me. Mama would have made
sure. And then again, perhaps she would have made me
go out there and stand up for myself.
The older bison were very kind to me. Many of them
were brothers and sisters and uncles and aunts. The
wolves sometimes came down to stalk us, mostly at calv-
ing time. Then the older bison would help the mothers
protect us. Once in a while the wolves did get one of us
but that was only if there was a sickness or injury that
made a calf unable to move quickly enough. And there
were grizzly bears who wandered into our territory,
tempted by the possibility of young buffalo venison. We
were taught always to keep watch no matter what we
were doing.
   But not even the older buffalo could give protection
when the buffalo hunters swooped down on us on
horseback. Then the whole herd would begin to move,

slowly at first but soon the prairies would echo with the thundering beat of our hooves. It was scary but exciting. Whenever this happened, Mama made sure we remained close together. The hunters used bows and arrows and they rode in among the running buffalo. If a hunter got close enough we could hear his hunting cries above the sounds of our hooves hitting earth. Sometimes they were silent, though, and all we could hear were heavy, labored breathing and the steady drumming of hoofbeats as the herd sought to put distance between itself and the danger.

Once, a horse and rider went down just in front to my left. I guess the horse must have stepped in a gopher hole. I heard both the horse and rider scream in agony as the buffalo behind pounded over them. I was glad I hadn't been behind them. It was all over very quickly which was probably fortunate for them. While there was danger to us from hunters, there was also danger to them. Once, I had seen a slow-moving wolf gored to death by a bull. Full-grown bison did not have many enemies to fear.

But full-grown bison had no defense against the two-legged hunters. On one of the hunts, an aunt went down with arrows lodged deep in the mass of her shaggy coat. When the hunters finally left us alone, everything began to quiet down. Many of the younger bison and a few of the older ones stopped to catch their wind and rest. My aunt's little calf, who was maybe a month younger than me, spent a long time crying for his Mama and wandering through the group, looking for her. When Mama finally realized that his mother was not coming back, she went to comfort and nurse my little cousin. His name was Bison Boy and he became my little brother.

He was the youngest of our whole group and also the smallest.

Big Ben and his friends were all older or bigger than Bison Boy and me. It was natural for them to want to bully us around. Because I was older than Bison Boy, it was my place to watch out for him. One day, I was returning from playing with some gophers when I was stopped in my tracks by Bison Boy's voice.

"Leave me alone. Please?" he was pleading in a small voice.

An uncle, unconcerned by their mischief, as we often developed our skills for defense by such play-fights, was grazing calmly. He stood between the group and me. Their attention was on Bison Boy and they did not notice me. As I watched, Big Ben and his friends took turns at battering Bison Boy from all sides. Bison Boy would go down and they'd wait for him to get up before one of them charged at him again. It was purely mean of them. It went beyond the usual head-butting. Now, Big Ben was older and bigger than me, as I said before, but I was mad. I charged out and aimed myself directly at Big Ben's shoulder. Big Ben, intent on Bison Boy, didn't see me coming until the last minute and by then it was too late. I hit him with my full weight and he went down. Before he could recover, I charged at him again. I bowled him over and this time he was able to get to his feet. He shook his head and looked at me. I was ready to charge again. Seeing my anger, he turned and trotted off.

The others, surprised by my intrusion, looked at Big Ben's departing form, then back at Bison Boy and me. I stood my ground, ready to accept any of their challenges. They made none and left to join Big Ben. I turned my attention to Bison Boy. He was having trouble getting up. One of his legs had been twisted or sprained. We didn't think it was broken but he could only limp painfully. For a youngster, or any animal, to be hurt was serious, very serious. Survival on the plains and in the wilderness meant one had to be fit at all times. Bison Boy and I knew this very well from our past observations. In his present condition, Bison Boy would be a prime target if the wolves came. What I had to do, and quickly, was to find Mama and bring her to Bison Boy. Just as I was about to leave, we heard sounds and I knew it was too late.

# CHAPTER 2

We all heard the whoops of the hunters before we saw them. Fortunately, Bison Boy and I were on the far side of the plain, opposite from where the riders came in. We were on the outskirts of our group, and nearby was a gully with a thick underbrush of willows. I urged Bison Boy to go down into the gully as the herd began to stampede. While we didn't have time to tell Mama what had happened, I was sure we soon would be back with the rest of the herd.

We heard the thundering of hooves and the hunting cries fade off into the distance. Then there was complete silence for a while before the birds and insects felt comfortable enough to begin making their various sounds. Both of us were trembling with nervousness. Never before had we been without the protection and security of Mama and our relatives. We were hidden for now from the hunters on horseback but what if the wolves came, or a grizzly bear? Or whatever else was out there waiting to dine on young fresh buffalo meat? Being the older one, I felt I had to hide my fear, pretend that everything would be okay. Bison Boy looked up to me as his protector now and I could see the trust in his eyes. He began to nibble at some grass, limping to new areas but always keeping me within his view. I watched and listened for signs of danger in all directions. The only noises were from the insects and the birds.

It was strange not to hear the snorting and occasional bellows of bison blowing dust from their noses. There were no sounds of swishing tails chasing flies away; no sounds of the shaking of great shaggy heads; no sounds of bison rolling on the earth to rub themselves or of hooves hitting the ground after scratching; no angry cows or bulls, stamping the ground in challenges. There were none of the sounds I had taken for granted until now. And I missed those sounds already. Without the great herd, the plains seemed totally empty.

Nighttime. It came too soon, too suddenly. Bison Boy had been trying to use his leg but I knew it was painful for him. I figured he ought to rest through the night and come morning, we would start out to search for the rest of the herd. The first night sound was of coyote yipping and howling but they were far off in the distance and soon only the crickets could be heard. Bison Boy lay down and went to sleep. I continued to stand guard. When morning came, I was surprised that nothing had happened during the night. Mama had told me that there were many night hunters and the safest place to be was as close to her as possible. If Bison Boy had known how much I had wanted to be with Mama, I don't think he would have felt so safe with me that first night, or the second or the third.

Slowly, we began to follow the trail of trampled grasses left by the herd. We soon had to hide all the time. Where the stampede had passed, the two-legged hunters' women and their children now were gathered around the carcasses of slain buffalo. While Bison Boy rested, I watched their movements. One group was working at removing a hide from a body while others cut the meat from a freshly stripped carcass into long flat pieces and lay them over rocks or hung them from sticks tied horizontally. I could see some of the children collecting wood for the fires the women had made near the bulky forms. We almost stumbled on a group of children who were picking berries. They were talking and laughing and seemed very harmless but I knew they could bring us down with their bows and arrows.

We detoured around them so we could continue our search. Maybe the night hunters also avoided the two-legged hunters. If so, the people hunters could give us protection for now. We rested at night as close as we dared to the campfires the people made. In the mornings, before any activity started, Bison Boy and I would leave without having been detected.

The days became weeks and the weeks became months. Signs of the herd were disappearing. We traveled slowly since Bison Boy's leg was still healing. There were less campfires and less activity on the plains from the two-legged hunters. Sometimes, we had to break from the cover of the trees and cross wide expanses of open prairie as we followed the difficult trail. Summer had turned into autumn. The grass was yellow and leaves of different colors fell to the ground. The bushes, bare of their foliage, no longer provided easy cover for us. There was a tense gray mood in the air, even on the sunny days, and it puzzled me. High in the skies, countless flocks of birds headed southward, leaving a quiet across the land. It was not a calm quiet but one that gave a sense of foreboding. Changes were coming. But what kind? The sense of being lost and alone deepened.

Bison Boy was still not fully recovered by the time the first snow came. We were both amazed by the white soft fluff that came down from above. We stuck our tongues out and the white snowflakes turned into raindrops on our tongues. We were quite fascinated those first few days. But then it became cold during the night, the coldest I ever felt, even though my shaggy coat had been growing in steadily during the last few months. Bison Boy and I tried to draw warmth from each other. On some of the following days, we were caught out in the open. The winds would howl around us, picking up the freshly fallen snow and swishing it around in mid-air. Maybe the winds and the snow played with each other as the birds and I had played. But I didn't think it was much fun. The air I breathed out became liquid like water, then froze the hair on my face and around my nostrils so that it hung down like icicles on tree branches. I sure missed my mother's warmth and I bet Bison Boy did, too, but he didn't complain and so neither did I.

By now, the signs of the herd had disappeared completely. Our initial search had become an aimless wandering as we concentrated more on looking for feeding areas. Sometimes, the sun would melt the snow. When it froze up again, we'd have to break through a hard crust of icy snow to reach the grasses. The wintery cold became milder, either because our full shaggy coats kept us warmer or because our bodies had adjusted to the lower temperatures. Now that the orchestra of the summer animals had departed for places unknown, we could hear individual sounds more clearly: the screech of an owl after its prey, squirrels bickering among themselves, and the fluttering wings of the snowbirds who stayed to brave this harsher season. We rarely saw any of the larger animals. I wondered where they all were.

Whenever the winds blew fiercely, we took refuge in the woods. One day, when we found such protection in a grove of brush and evergreens, a scent came to us which sent chills down our backs. One of the big cats, who normally lived up in the mountains across the plains, was somewhere closeby. Mama had said that long harsh winters usually forced them to the lower lands. It must have circled around us because everywhere we turned, we could smell its scent.

"Bison Boy, you'd better hide in that thick shrub over there. I'll stay here in the open and try to distract him," I said.

"Are you sure?" he asked, concerned for my safety.

"I'm sure," I said, showing more bravado than I felt.

Bison Boy, as lame as he was, wouldn't stand a chance. I watched him make his way to the hiding spot, wishing I could go along, too. But I knew that I had a better chance of driving any animal away. I circled and made noises to draw attention away from Bison Boy and to make myself ready for battle. Suddenly, a loud shrill scream pierced the air. Startled, I jumped, must have been four feet in the air. At the same time, the cougar pounced on my back, a savage fury of needled claws digging through my winter shag. I was terrified. All my cool, well-planned strategy vanished instantly. I bucked, I turned, I twisted, trying in vain to get my horns into him. There was no way I could drive away an

animal that was firmly attached to my back. I knew I had to stay up because if I didn't, if I went down, I would never get up. I felt a warm wetness trickle down my sides. Worse than that, I felt myself tiring from both his weight and my futile attempts to ward him off.

Above the cat's ear-splitting screams, I heard the sound of a thunderclap. Then the raging beast went limp, slipped from my back silently, hit the ground and didn't move. I had been waiting for such a chance. I turned on it with my own fury of wounded pride and pounded it with my hooves, then I gored it with my short horns.

I realized it wasn't fighting back or making any attempts to run away. I poked at it, trying to figure out its sudden change. The sound of a horse impatiently shaking its head made me look up. Bison Boy was still out of sight but there on a horse was a young, fair-skinned man. He was watching me. I knew then that he had saved my life.

"Holy cow, I heard that there were white buffalo around, but I ain't never seen one before," he said in a surprised voice. "Are you okay?" He urged his horse in closer. Immediately, I backed away from him.

"It's okay, I'm not going to hurt you. Heck, I saved your life, didn't I?" he said.

I stopped but eyed him warily. I didn't want to seem ungrateful but Mama had told me that people were to be avoided.

The man dismounted and bent over the cat. "He's a big one. You're lucky I was passing through this way, you know that? I'm on my way to the mountains, that's where I'm going. I been there once when I was small and there's no place like it. That is if you don't run into no trouble. I reckoned on becoming a mountain man.

Maybe I'll just look for gold or maybe I'll just scout around and discover places no man's been before. White men, anyways.''

While he talked, he loaded the cougar onto the back of his protesting horse. Then he got back on. "Well, got to get going. You take care of yourself, hear? I won't always be around to save your hide.''

With that, he reined his horse around and was gone as suddenly as he had come.

I called out to Bison Boy, who came out in the open. He asked, "Are you all right? Maybe I should have tried to help?''

"No, you did right to stay hidden. I'm okay,'' I said.

Bison Boy worried about my wounds but I thought I would probably be wearing the scars with pride.

"I felt like a coward,'' he said quietly.

"Same here.''

"You did? But you stayed and fought,'' he said with admiration.

"Tried to fight,'' I corrected. "Anyways, sometimes, it's braver to hide. And smarter. Next time, I plan to be smarter.'' I gave a last look at the spot where I almost went down and then we left.

After that experience, we made an even more serious attempt to locate the herd. Our efforts were soon rewarded. We came upon a clearing where we saw in the disturbed snow recent signs that many buffalo had fed. Excitement hit both of us at the same time. As we followed this new trail, the bison scent grew stronger. I called out when we heard the sounds of other buffalo. The answering call was not familiar but when we topped the hill we were climbing, there below was the glorious sight of a multitude of bison, many of them looking up towards us. From our stand, we called to Mama. A group of the bison broke through the herd and came towards us.

Mama was as happy to see us as we were to see her. Even the old-time bullies were glad and very curious as to what had happened to us. Bison Boy told them all about our adventures, embellishing the account of our encounter with the cougar and the man. This reunion made our precarious adventures all worthwhile. For the moment, I wanted never to be separated from Mama or the herd again.

# CHAPTER 3

Seasons passed. I grew very large, though not as large as Big Ben. My shaggy coat was almost white, like snow. Because we had survived our first year, and shouldn't have, Bison Boy and I had attained a grander stature. Mama said that we would never become herd leaders because we were not aggressive enough. While cows sometimes became herd leaders, I knew I did not have the disposition to lead. I always thought if anyone were to lead from our age group, most likely it would be Big Ben. His size alone would make him leader, and he certainly was aggressive enough. Bison Boy and I would be happy to be followers.

By this time, Mama had given birth to two others and now I had two younger sisters. They were a year apart. I had become their protectors as my older brothers and sisters had been mine. Mama didn't talk to me as much as she had when I was being taught by her. Perhaps I would soon be mothering my own.

As I grew older, I experienced continual changes. Unlike my first winter season, I no longer had that sense of foreboding when seasons changed. In springtime, when we shed our winter coats, we couldn't scratch enough. I thought spring must be the most uncomfortable season. But on hot summer days, I changed my mind and decided that summer was the most uncomfortable season. On the whole, most of the changes were expected and I really did not have many complaints.

One of the changes that startled us all was the way the two-legged hunters hunted. They had always come down on their horses and used bows and arrows, silent weapons. The only noise they made was a low whistling sound. I heard the sound a few times as arrows flew close by me.

Different hunters now came with different weapons. 'Muzzle-loading rifles', they were called. The riders still had to come in among the herd to shoot at us and when they did, loud thunderclap noises sounded out. I soon knew if such a weapon was aimed at a certain bison and the noise sounded, that bison would go down under the rush of the stampede behind him.

One time a rider poured some gun powder into the muzzle, then spit in small steel balls from his mouth, pounded the rifle butt against his saddle and aimed it at one of the cows. He pulled the trigger. When the gunblast sounded, it blew the rider right off his horse. I think I was the only bison who ever took note of all these details because when I would mention them later, no one, not even Bison Boy, had noticed what I did.

Next to our fear of the hunters with those rifles, we were afraid of prairie fires. It seemed they could sweep across the plains faster than an owl could swoop in on a mouse. One day, the herd was grazing calmly when the first whiff of smoke came to us. We immediately became anxious. Was it the man-made fire or was it the prairie fire? We stood alert, watching. Sure enough, other animals came into view. Blindly, they passed us by, and went on down to the river east of us. Antelope, bears, lynx, a couple of mountain lions, and elk raced by, no longer the hunters or the hunted. Overhead, birds flew, chased from their nests in the grasses or the trees. All had wild, desperate looks in their eyes. We decided it was high time we headed for the river. The fire was far enough away that we didn't panic but we did separate into smaller groups. I was in the lead of our group.

Up ahead, directly in our path, a single rider seemed to appear from nowhere. He was having trouble controlling his horse. The horse reared and stumbled, throwing the rider off. Before he could remount, the horse bolted towards the river. There was something vaguely familiar about the man. As we got closer, I saw him look towards us. There was no place where he could run for protection. We would be upon him in either direction. Then I remembered who he was. He was the fair-skinned boy, now a man, who had saved me from the cougar. I slowed my gait, forcing the others behind me to slow down or detour around me. I could do this only because my group hadn't panicked.

Fortunately, the man saw me and stayed where he was. I was able to block the rest of the herd from stampeding him to a pulp. When the last ones had gone around me, I joined them. We weren't very far from the river now. We all swam to the other side and rested. I looked back across the river and saw the man catch his horse. He got on, then looked at me, waved and rode off along the river bank on the other side.

Over the next few years, different kinds of weapons were used. And it came to me that I could no longer call the men who used them 'hunters'. Our first encounter with them occurred on the southern ranges. The horsemen who came no longer had to ride in among us. They rode on the outskirts, safe from falling under the hooves of the buffalo, and shot at us, indiscriminately. They never stayed long and they never came with their women and children following behind them. Often, in the past, I had parted from the herd, curious about others who shared the plains with us. Once, I had watched a small buffalo group being stampeded right off a cliff to their death. It had seemed very cruel at that time but at least women and children had been there to harvest those who had been killed. We had been hunted in different ways but never had we seen this kind of outright killing before.

Having drifted southward over the winter, we were beginning the long trek north for the summer grasses. I think we all thought there would be safety from those rifles. But all through those days the raids continued, forcing us in other directions. Sometimes, the riders still rode in and out of the herd and, sometimes, they used different types of weapons. By now, the stampeding was no longer just frenzied excitement. There was a dreadful fear among all of us.

On one lightning-fast raid, there was not only fear but a great sense of loss. My sire, Great Bison, was shot. One minute, he had been running along beside me. The next, he cried out, bellowing his pain and rage, then went down beneath the onrush of a thousand hooves.

Sporadic raids continued over the next few days,

keeping us on the move. While death was accepted as a part of our life, there was always a sense of loss if a relative or friend went missing. Usually, we never went back on the trail looking, but one night, curiosity forced me to leave my group to go back on our trail to look for my sire. By then, the raids had ceased.

As I was making my way through another group, Bison Boy spotted me and called out to me. "Are you going somewhere?" he asked.

"My sire went down and I'm going to look for him," I answered.

"Could I go with you?" he asked.

"You'd better stay here. Just in case anything more happens. Watch out for Mama and our sisters."

"Well, okay," he said reluctantly.

I left alone. By now, I knew the general trails of my herd and didn't have to worry about losing them again. I traveled southward all night, staying to the cover of the trees and bushes whenever possible. By morning, I began to see the remains of dead bison littered across the plains. But unlike most times before, there were no two-legged people harvesting the carcasses. The lifeless forms just lay about, looking abandoned. I went back along the trail until I came to the spot where I thought Great Bison had gone down. I spotted his still form before I realized it was him. By now, in the mid-day's heat, flies were all over him, on his glazed open eyes, around his nostrils and mouth where his tongue was swollen and lolling out the side closest to the ground, but they were especially thick around the blood spot in his side. The blood was reddish-brown, dried hard. It was the first time I saw death like this.

Where did the flies come from, anyway? How did they know to come? Did they smell death better than we did? Flies bothered us but not as great in number and not the kind that swarmed here, around this death. I shook my head and pawed the ground to make the flies go away. They rose in the air in a large cluster, probably angry at me for disturbing their . . . what? Their feast? I stood over the corpse of my sire, not knowing for sure what to do next. The flies settled back down on the carcass until I disturbed them again.

All of a sudden, I realized there was another living presence nearby. I snorted and turned in surprise, trying to identify what the presence might be and bracing myself for whatever might happen.

# CHAPTER 4

A dark-skinned man stood near some shrubs. He was watching me with an expression of awe and surprise. I saw that he had a bow and arrows in a pouch on his back but he made no attempt to set them up. It seemed to me that we stood there for hours looking at each other. What I sensed most from him was sadness. Could he be sad for my sire?

I didn't think so, for his kind, they with their bows and arrows, had often hunted mine in the past. They hunted us for food as we hunted new grass growth for our food. It was simply a life-cycle. They probably did not mourn for us as we did not mourn for the grasses we ate. So what could he be sad about? I did not understand. I did not fear him, either. I sensed that for now he was not a hunter. But the expression on his face puzzled me.

"Are you for real, White Buffalo?" he said in a low voice, almost like a whispering breeze.

I wondered how he knew my name. Although he did not talk as Bison Boy and I talked, I could understand what he was saying.

"Grandfather said they would come to kill your kind so that they could conquer our kind. They have begun, haven't they?" he said, looking over the field of dead bison.

Still in a soft voice, he asked, "Why do you stand over that bull in particular, White Buffalo?"

He began to approach me, cautiously. Somehow I knew that if I had charged and killed him, he would have accepted that as an honorable death. I had no intentions of charging. I knew also that if he got close enough, he would touch me. I feared that, yet I anticipated what it might feel like to be touched by our most feared enemy—man. I stood my ground, overcoming my instinct to flee. Slowly, he took a step at a time. I waited. His hand was extended towards me. I sniffed at it without moving my head, my eyes watching his every move. Finally his hand touched my nostrils and he scratched my head, still talking in a subdued tone. I was surprised that it felt good to be scratched like that. At first I had wanted to shake off the feeling but I knew that a sudden movement from me would frighten him. He scratched along my side as he spoke. He said his name was Lone Wolf. I thought to myself that he didn't look like a lone wolf, he looked like a man.

After a while, I turned my attention back to my sire and to the business of keeping the flies off him. High above, the vultures were circling. They had been here

when I arrived, also knowing death had come to this particular valley.

Lone Wolf began digging in the ground while I stood looking on, curious about what he was doing and why. It took him a long time, way past dusk, and finally, he gave up for the night. He slept on the ground near me, so I settled down, too. In the morning, he returned to his task of digging. The hole he was making next to my sire was very large and quite deep. When he finished digging, he climbed out, went to the other side of my sire's carcass and pushed at it as hard as he could. I could see his muscles straining. Unable to budge my sire, he went back to digging, almost taking the ground right out from under the body. When he had dug enough, he went around the body and pushed again. This time, the carcass gave way and rolled into the hole. Then he piled the earth back on top of it until there was a mound of earth but no carcass. He had buried my sire's body completely!

The flies left, probably for some other carcass beyond. I realized that neither the flies, nor the vultures, would be able to get at my sire's body now. I was grateful to the man who called himself Lone Wolf.

"There. How is that, my friend? You do not have to chase those flies away now. And the vultures will not feast off his meat. And maybe, in the future sometime, if we want to meet we can come here and wait." He wiped his hands on his clothing and came over to rub the side of my face with tenderness. I was in awe of him as well as grateful.

"I must get back to my people, now. We will meet again some day, my friend." With that, he put his pouch and food pack over his shoulder and left.

I watched him disappear among the bushes. I made
my own way back to my herd. When I told Bison Boy
about my strange encounter, he was full of concern for
my sanity. Never ever would he let a man get that close
to him, let alone touch him. He thought I must be either
the most courageous buffalo ever or the most foolish.
We laughed as he teased me about the probability of my
being the most foolish. But long after that meeting, I
thought about Lone Wolf and I hoped we would meet
again, soon.

# CHAPTER 5

More seasons passed; springs, when the last of the young were born; summers, when it was hot and tempers flared more readily; autumns, when we concentrated on fattening ourselves on grasses in preparation for the winters, which were always lean times for all the creatures, big and small. More and more often, parties of hunters with their deafening rifles broke the calm on the prairies. Sometimes, there were the mile-long caravans of the hunters who still harvested the meat. They were always interesting to watch and if they camped overnight they filled the prairie with the sounds of their music and laughter. They came with their families in wagons that made the most horrible screeching noises, worse than the sounds of screaming mountain lions. Once they were on the move, I put as much distance between their ear-piercing wagons and myself as possible. But the hunters who disturbed us the most were those who came only to shoot us down.

The land upon which we lived was so large that we

could travel in circles for months and never come upon the same feeding ranges again. But one day, when we were on the southern ranges, we came across double steel rails on the ground which cut right across our path. The leader snorted and sniffed and pawed the ground, fearful of the strange change. We all stayed where we were on the north side of the train tracks for days but the instinct to go south finally overcame our reluctance and our leader led us across.

All through that winter, we lost many of our own to the rifle-bearing hunters. It was at this time that I thought not to call them 'hunters' anymore. To me, hunters had been people or animals who hunted for food, who couldn't live without the hunt. Sport, murder, those were words we had never really known before. Once in a while, an animal might become very, very sick in the mind, sometimes in the body, and they might kill another animal and not for food. They would leave the food. Or an animal might kill another in the mating seasons. Or they might kill another animal over food, protection of their young or their possessions. Sometimes, an animal's murderous instincts were built into it and other animals knew this and expected it. There were enough legitimate reasons for killing. Men had hunted us for food and that was acceptable. But what some of the rifle-carrying men were doing, that was murder.

The following summer, I left the herd and traveled alone to the meeting place arranged by Lone Wolf. I had come to distrust and fear man so I was both anxious and afraid to see Lone Wolf again. His kind of men were not the ones who had hunted us mercilessly, so I still had faith in him. I didn't have to wait near the mound for long. He soon arrived on horseback.

"I had a dream you would be here. So I came," he said, after dismounting. He came towards me.

He touched me again but this time I quivered. "You have been through much, my friend. And so have I. Things are not good for my people. They want us to sign treaties that say we will live on reservations and that we will not hunt anymore. How can we live if we cannot hunt? Some of the nations have signed these treaties and now they depend on the white man for their food. And they are hungry. There is talk of war among my people. War. That may be the only way to protect your kind. But some of the chiefs say that our way of life is changing. That we must change with them. Or die. They say the soldiers will kill all of your kind, if we don't give up our ideas of fighting for our lands. Our chief thinks that we must not give up. He says we must fight and die fighting if we must. I will follow where our chief leads. I have seen what is happening. The changes. I see your herd pass by and I see that there are less and less. If these are the kinds of changes that we are supposed to accept without question. . . ." Lone Wolf shook his head, as if there were no choices left to him.

I sensed he was sadder than before, much sadder. I suddenly became angry for him. I shook my head and pawed the ground. That was all I could do. Who could fight those murder weapons? Who could stop the loss of our kind? Times were changing, but not for the better. There would be no room for our kind in the changed world in the future. Iron tracks cutting across our lands. Barbed wires that had to be toppled so we could make our way to our feeding grounds. Those strange hairless buffalo eating our grasses. Where did they come from, anyway? Would the men with their weapons always,

always in the future make changes for the worst? Did they not care about their futures? Would this land of ours one day be covered by men murdering each other?

Lone Wolf paced about like a trapped animal, angrily talking about the loss of control by the Indian nations. "I am sorry for talking so. I did not want to meet you again just to talk about the sadness which fills my heart. I wanted to talk about good things. I wanted to see how you were. I wanted to tell you that I am glad of our friendship. It helps to know that your spirit is with me, White Buffalo."

He came back and scratched me again on my shoulder and by now I felt relaxed, all qualms gone about this man at least. I nuzzled him as gently as I could to try to communicate that I had mutual feelings. I wanted to tell him that I understood. I had seen more of my group gone, just like my sire who lay in the mound nearby. But no one had buried them, or even harvested them. Lone Wolf talked of hunger. Far away, there probably had been meat enough to last his family a lifetime. But it had not been harvested. We had seen the remains: rotting bodies covered with flies and maggots; so many carcasses that even the vultures hadn't been able to keep up. I wanted to tell him, if I could go to war with him, I would gladly have done so. But how could we fight back? We were powerless, capable only of running. But there would come a time when there would not even be places to run to.

Lone Wolf made a fire and cooked a meal over it. Afterward, he continued sitting, sometimes talking and other times, being silent. We both remained very still, listening, thinking. The crackling of the fire eventually died out. Nearby, his horse fed, grinding grass between its teeth. Once, a hawk, far above us, called out. A bumblebee noisily skimmed by us, and then there was silence again. This stillness was comforting. It was peaceful. Peace. There was not much of that left for us, these days. Too soon, Lone Wolf prepared to leave. Our reunion had been somber, though peaceful. One day, we would be able to meet here and we'd both be happy.

More seasons passed. I met Lone Wolf again. This was not the happy reunion for which I had hoped. Lone Wolf told me two of his children had starved to death. A small, desperate band of younger warriors had gone out on their own and had raided some stores and some homes. They had been caught by the white men and they had all been hung. Fourteen desperate men—who had hunted for food. Lone Wolf told me also about a disease that had come to his kind of people in a far-away place. The disease was called smallpox. It had gone through their camps swiftly, killing the already hungry and weakened people. When Lone Wolf told me about these things I felt more sympathy for him than I did for myself and my kind. I nuzzled him some more in an attempt to comfort him.

The time came for us to part. This time I worried for Lone Wolf. As far as he knew, the time was drawing close for his people to go to war against the soldiers who wanted control and would do anything to get it. Lone Wolf was no longer the strong young warrior I had met the first time years ago. Lone Wolf seemed bent of spirit which gave him more age than he ought to have. I really wished that I could do something, anything. But what man did, I could not physically control or influence. In recent years, our own number had been getting smaller. I now understood that control of our numbers would give control over the Indian nations. They could not kill us all, I reckoned. But maybe I reckoned wrong.

# CHAPTER 6

Our wandering to search for fresh food ranges took us southward again. By now, we had become more accustomed to the two steel lines that cut across our circular path. The whole herd was on either side of the lines the day the beast came down and separated us for good. Our group was still on the north side. Never had we been so terrified as on that day. Not only was this beast hundreds of times larger than the biggest grizzly bear, but from its sides sounded the deafening thunderclaps like the rifles made. Almost at the same time that the living, pulsing horror hissed down the two tracks, men on horseback came from all directions. And all their weapons were being fired at us.

Our own direction was unfocused. Every time we headed one way we were driven back in on ourselves. It was brutal for the very young buffalo because they often were pounded on, sometimes by their own mothers. Thousands of volleys of deadly bullets found their fatal marks and thousands of bison went down within an hour. Even though there was so much dying for us, they didn't let up. Wave after wave of bullets stopped us from escaping. I constantly expected that one or even a few of them would find their marks in me. I knew from the cries of those who were hit that there was pain. The smell of blood was everywhere I turned. The cool instinct to survive in the wilderness did not count for anything at this place on this day. We were all in a frenzy of panic. My group was no longer together and I didn't know what had happened to any of them.

I heard my mother then. She was making enraged noises but suddenly the cry changed to one of agony and I knew she had been hit more than once. By the time I found her, she was lying on her side, her breath making horrible strangled noises, her eyes wild with fright. I nuzzled her and it seemed to calm her a little. She looked at me then, questioningly, wondering as I was, why?

She lay there breathing more quietly, waiting perhaps for death to bring her relief. I stood over her, waiting with her. By now the surviving buffalo had made their break northward and most of the horsemen had ridden off after them. My mother, feeling a strong need to go with the rest of the herd, attempted to stand up but fell back.

One of the horsemen seemed to be talking to the beast, which had now stopped in its tracks. He spotted my mother and spurred his horse towards us. When he raised his rifle to point it at her, I charged. His horse reared and bolted to avoid me. The rider, unprepared for its sudden action, fell off his horse. I stopped and

waited to see what he would do. He walked over to his
rifle, picked it up and pointed it at my mother once
again. Incredibly, he completely ignored me. I lowered
my head and charged again. The thud that sounded
when I hit him was the last sound he ever heard. Mean-
while, my mother had stood up and was trembling on
shaky legs.

More horsemen came down from the direction of the
beast. I saw them raise their rifles and aim them at
Mama. I knew I couldn't cover the distance to stop
them. I heard the shots ring out, then their victory yells.
With dread I turned around to look at Mama. She was
all bloodied. This time she hadn't made a sound when
she'd been hit. They kept pouring bullets into her as
they rode in crazy circles. I thought there was no sense
in charging any of them. My Mama was past defending.

The buffalo 'hunters', as I heard them call each
other, also ignored me completely as if they hadn't seen
me or didn't think I was a good enough buffalo to kill.
Once they had destroyed my mother, they rode off
laughing and saying how good they felt, what great
hunters they were, that shooting buffalo from a train
was an experience everyone should have.

As with my father, I stood by my mother's body for a
long time. I slept through the first night, dreaming of
the old times when we were all much younger and when
there was a natural way of life on the prairies, with no
trains, no tracks, none of the barbed-wire fences. They
were days when the land was wide-open and free. I woke
up many times during the night and when I looked
towards the train, I could see it still, not hissing and
flaring anymore. Perhaps it was pacified now. It did not
leave its two iron tracks to feast on the buffalo carcasses. Nor did any of the people come away from it to

harvest the meat. I could hear laughter and loud talk emitting from the interior of the monster. I recalled Lone Wolf telling me about fire-water. He had said it was evil. It changed people—for the worse. I wondered if the beast had this fire-water. Uneasily, I drifted back to sleep.

The next day was hot. I could tell from the early morning sun that it would be one of the hottest days yet. The monster on the tracks began moving. I watched warily for signs of its coming toward me. I thought perhaps I should charge it, and if it killed me, it would be worth it. But then who would watch over Mama? Who would chase the flies away that were already beginning to come? I let it go by without doing anything. Soon the prairie was quiet.

This time it was a deathly quiet, with only the sounds of the flies. Later, the vultures circled high but only briefly. They were soon down at the carcasses, gorging themselves.

By late evening, I was forced to leave my mother's side to go for water. My tongue felt swollen and the water that night was the first sense of relief I'd had since the coming of the beast. When I finished, I went back to where my mother lay. I ate nearby but very little. That night, I slept without dreaming.

The next few days I wandered off to eat and drink away from the rotting carcasses. I felt sick but my determination to stay by my mother's body overcame my desire to get away from the stench and horror. Even my mother's carcass had begun to rot and, again, I felt frustrated and powerless to do anything about it.

The days I remained there turned into weeks but for some reason I felt compelled to stay. I had hoped somehow that even though he was far north, Lone Wolf

would come down here and bury my mother's body. I waited but he did not come. By now, I had also been thinking more and more about Bison Boy and the rest of my relatives. I had come across some of them and I did not wonder about them. Their carcasses were rotting quickly in the heat of the days. They were barely recognizable by now. By the end of that horrible summer, the bones had been stripped clean by the vultures, the coyote, the foxes and the insects. My last sight was of a vast field as far as the eye could see, covered with white bleached bones, the humble remnants of once proud and mighty animals. Our territory was diminishing in size and population.

If I had known there would be more seasons like the one I had just been through, I think I would gladly have charged that beast when I had the chance to do so. The summer in the north was spent with the herd I had rejoined, searching for food. Prairie fires had wiped out many of our usual feeding places. Never before had the fires been so destructive as the year after the first great train massacre.

I had met again with Lone Wolf and he knew what had happened to our herd in the south. Somehow, he knew that I had waited for him in vain and he said he had wanted to join me but it had been impossible. He told me that his wife had died and that now his family was all gone, he would have nothing to lose when his people went to war. I knew what war meant. Sometimes two bulls would war with each other for some cows. Sometimes the winner of the war turned out to be the loser. One year, Big Ben won his war and got himself some rangy mean-tempered cows. Bison Boy and I had ribbed Big Ben over his great 'victory'. I wished I could tell Lone Wolf about it and lighten his mood. Even people ought to be able to laugh once in a while.

When I went to meet Lone Wolf, Bison Boy came along but he quickly retreated once he saw the man come towards us. We spent the night and part of the next day together, he talking and I listening. He talked of his people, of their past, and of his great chief who led them now. Then it was time for us to part. I watched him walk away, already missing him. What if another of my relatives was killed, who would bury the body? And while I hated and feared mankind, Lone Wolf was the single exception. I was fascinated by him. I liked how he talked to me as if he knew I could understand his every word. I liked how he scratched me around my face and sides. He had such a gentle spirit. But he was going to war. As I watched him walk away, I thought again how aged he had become.

# CHAPTER 7

Slowly, I turned and joined Bison Boy waiting off in the distance, out of sight. We started back to the herd which was down in a valley. I stood on the crest of a hill, looking down at what remained of us. I was startled. No longer were there millions of us. One more onslaught by those men with their rifles and I figured we would all be wiped out. As I had known long ago, Big Ben had become the herd leader. Miraculously, the three of us were among last year's survivors. None of us held Big Ben accountable for the killings against us. No leader was expected to provide safety under the conditions which had befallen us. I did suggest to Big Ben that we be more cautious than ever before and hide ourselves as much as possible, even if it meant smaller groupings and hiding in the cover of the trees and the bushes. We still traveled together but at the first sound or sight of any man, we split up and moved for cover. Once in a while a whole group of buffalo was found and shot but in that season, the killings were not as numerous as they had been before.

We were in the general area where Lone Wolf and his people often traveled, making their camps, then moving on. I was surprised when on our next visit, he brought along two small children, a boy-child and a girl-child.

"These are the children of my brother and his wife, White Buffalo. I brought them here so they could see the great white buffalo and so that your spirit would pass on down through them to their young ones. I am getting old and my time to die will soon come," he said, running his hand across my shoulder to show the children they ought not to be afraid of me.

The children had stood back shyly and then they came and petted me. I lowered my head to sniff at their hands and I stood very still so I wouldn't frighten them. The girl-child bent to pull up some grasses to feed to me. Their touches were very soft. The respect they showed me made me feel very special.

"The next time we see each other, my friend, I will have gone to war. There has been a gathering of great chiefs. Our chief told of a vision he had." He looked off into the distance, as if his destination was there in the far-away lands. The time came for them to leave. When the three of them disappeared, I knew I would not see Lone Wolf again or feel his hand on my face and shoulders.

We were on the move again, going further north. Day and night, I thought mostly of Lone Wolf. Finally, I stopped and let the herd go on without me. I turned back in a southward direction. Since our first encounter with the train I had come to realize that most men could not see me, except Lone Wolf and the two children. So I did not need the protection of the herd. Many times I had come upon man and knew I could watch him without his being able to see me. So on the day that I approached the sounds of war cries and gunfire, I did not fear for my own safety.

I knew immediately what was going on. It was the war of which Lone Wolf had talked. I saw the bodies of warriors, soldiers and horses lying in a valley. I was drawn closer to the river where the sounds were louder. From a hill, which enabled me to see far in all directions, I watched for a while. The Indians greatly outnumbered the soldiers, although one group of soldiers had hidden themselves in some brushwood. Indians on horseback scouted nearby, seeking them out. Dust hung heavy in the air as the warriors' horses pranced about, kicking up the sandy soil. The warriors set fire to the dry brush. Under the cover of the thick smoke, the soldiers, hiding behind an overturned tree trunk, cleared the area around them of grass and brush. I thought that with so many warriors and so few soldiers, this war should have ended quickly. Maybe the warriors were toying with the soldiers.

I watched closely for Lone Wolf and thought that he might see me up here on this hill. Far to my left, I saw a large camp with women and children rushing about. It seemed to me that they were making preparations to leave. Suddenly on the next hill, a lone rider appeared. I wondered if he was the great warrior chief that Lone Wolf had told me about. I watched him as he surveyed the scene below us, perhaps so intently that he did not notice me. At first, he seemed satisfied with what was going on, but then he showed disgust. I looked below in time to see an Indian, not of Lone Wolf's people, hiding in the thickets beside the soldiers. Finally, the lone rider turned his horse away from me and started down the hill in the other direction. When he had gone, I decided that I might as well return north to join the herd. Lone Wolf had gone to war and there was nothing I could do anymore. It appeared that his people had won.

Not long after their war, we suffered through more of the ravaging attacks on our diminishing herd. I escaped any kind of physical injury but both Bison Boy and Big Ben were killed. Their loss was as great a blow to me as if I had been hit.

Big Ben took many bullets but before he died, he charged blindly at one of his attackers, killing the soldier and maiming his mount so that the horse had to be shot as well.

Bison Boy's death came later. The soldiers did not press on after us and when we felt safe enough to stop, I discovered Bison Boy had been wounded a few times. He was maddened by his pain and charged all others who came close. He kept tossing his head until dizziness brought him to his knees. All through that night, he was driven to a frenzy by his wounds. He suffered in silence. We heard only the sounds of his agonized movements.

By the time the sun began to rise, he had grown weak from the loss of his blood. I licked the wounds on his back and that seemed to soothe him. We both knew he was dying. Finally, he lay down quietly. In the end, he raised his head to nuzzle me briefly, then calmly laid his head on the ground and died.

I bellowed out long and loud in futile protest. The sound echoed across the plains, up and down the valleys, and reverberated again and again. That day, I began to feel a numbness about life. I recalled how Big Ben and I had started out. We'd been adversaries, but we had become close friends over the years. And Bison Boy had been more like a brother, always loyal and gentle. Now they, like my mother and sire, were gone.

Both of them had sired many. They had been good protectors of their families. But in spite of that, most of their offspring were also gone. Too many times, calves and heifers hadn't lived beyond their first year because too many times, their mothers had been killed. I had never produced offspring although I had helped others in the protection of their young. I was now the oldest of what was left of our herd. I no longer stood over the bodies of those who were close to me. It had come to me that I was protecting only the dead when I could not even protect the living.

That morning we continued on our way, listlessly. In the following days, we fed, we traveled, we went to watering places, we continued with our lives. I sometimes longed to go my own way as I had in the past. But to where? It was a longing that happened only in my mind. Sometimes, my tired, aching body just wanted to lie down somewhere and stay put. Sometimes, I'd dream and I'd feel great anger. Sometimes, I didn't dream but just wished I could be in another place at another time. Awake, I always felt lonely. Lone Wolf had said his time to die would come soon. His body must have been among those other bodies, on the battlefield. I wondered if the warriors had won. And if so, what had they won? This land was no longer ours. Another kind of animal was taking it over. I wished I were younger and then maybe I could do battle with it. I didn't know what to make of all that was happening. Maybe I was too old to think anymore. I had lost my curiosity about life on the plains. Maybe my own time to die had come.

# CHAPTER 8

There were days that I thought about Lone Wolf. I hoped he wasn't dead so I could see him one more time. Finally, having convinced myself that he was still alive, I left the group and went on my own to look for him. I waited at the mound where my sire had been buried, and in the following days, I fed and went to the watering hole not far away. I stayed because, wherever Lone Wolf was, he would know somehow that I was waiting. I heard the sounds of hoofbeats before the men came into view. At first, I thought it was Lone Wolf. Perhaps he had brought the children with him. I was glad. I wanted to see them, too, one more time. Instead, four men dressed in the soldier uniforms rode into view. I made no attempt to hide because I thought they couldn't see me. But this time, I thought wrong!

"Well, will you look at that?" said the first soldier.

"Wowee! A white buffalo!" the second soldier exclaimed.

"I heard tell that there were some but I never believed it. That hide will bring in a lot of money," said the third.

"Why do you suppose it's standing over there? Why doesn't it run?" asked the second man.

"Aw, who cares? Let's get it!" said the third man.

"Hey, do you suppose they get white at a certain age? Maybe she's . . . how old do buffalo get, anyhow?" asked the fourth soldier, as he raised his rifle.

The others also raised their rifles and aimed at me. I felt the first bullet burn its way through my chest. The impact threw me back off-balance and I went down. But I quickly got back up, just as another bullet slammed into my shoulder. I stumbled and got up once again. I had to get away from them, but before I could take a single step, another bullet made a burning path through my body. The pain was as bad and hurtful as I thought it must be. I staggered but was able to remain standing.

Just then, an Indian rode towards us, his horse at full gallop. He was shouting and shooting his rifle at the soldiers. I saw one fall from his horse. The others aimed their rifles at the Indian as he raced to reach us. That gave me momentary strength to charge. I hit one horse in the shoulder before it realized I was coming. Both the horse and rider went down. Another shot rang out and I was hit again.

Through the haze of pain I was feeling, I heard gunshots coming from far-off behind me. I saw another of the soldiers fall from his horse, his blue shirt now turning a shiny crimson red. Just like when they shot Mama and all the others of my kind. The last one fell and he, too, became covered with his own blood. Soon all four were lying on the ground, either dead or dying. I stumbled over to where Lone Wolf had fallen from his horse. He had been shot in the head and in the chest. The weight of my body hit the ground with a thud as I lay down near Lone Wolf to rest my head near his. I could hear the sounds of more horses approaching. . . .

* * *

Two horsemen rode up to where the buffalo, the Indian and the four soldiers lay.

"They killed her," said the fair-skinned, older man. He usually made his home in the mountains with his friend, a Metis from the north. He remained on his horse and stared at the scene before him.

"For its hide, no doubt. Or maybe just for the sport," said the big Metis. He dismounted to take a closer look. "Hey, this here's that Lone Wolf!" he exclaimed. "He should of stayed north with the rest of the Sioux. Can't figure out why he'd come back here."

"They look like they were friends," said the fair-skinned man, thoughtfully.

"A buffalo and a man? Heat's gotten to you. It's a pity, though. Bet you these soldiers were out scouting for Indians, eh?" The Metis got back on his horse and prepared to ride off. "Well, we'd better high-tail it out of here. Before any more of them soldiers come. They'll blame us for killing all five of them, both the soldiers and Lone Wolf."

"Wait! We can't just leave them there. Out in the open," said the fair-skinned man.

"What do you want to do? You can lift that buffalo onto your horse, can you? I got some news for you, *mon ami*. Your horse couldn't stand its weight," the Metis said, grinning.

The other man thought about this for a moment and then, suddenly inspired, said, "We'll bury them! Together. Side by side. Two friends should be laid to rest, side by side."

"Are you crazy? We couldn't dig a hole big enough for that buffalo. Besides them soldiers could come any time," the Metis said, his grin gone. He searched the distance for signs that his prediction might come true that moment.

"Well, I'm not leaving until they're buried. That's it. You going to help me or not?" the other one asked. He dismounted and looked up at his friend.

"I don't know why it is that you're so crazy. I don't know why I'm crazy enough to travel with you, either." The Metis scratched his head, looking very puzzled.

"You go back to the wagon and get the shovels. I'll stay here. If them soldiers came, they'd take the hide and think nothing of it."

"Could you blame them? If we weren't such crazy fools, we'd take the hide ourselves instead of burying it." The Metis shook his head.

"Go on, get the shovels, will you," the other said as he looked over at the buffalo and the Indian.

"Bury a buffalo. Who ever heard of burying a buffalo?" grumbled the Metis, as he rode off towards their camp.

After he was gone, the fair-skinned man walked over to the bodies and bent down to touch the white bison. "It is you, isn't it? It's been a lifetime since I last saw you. But your spirit has always been with me. You've made me feel special. And you gave me a longer life, too. For both of those things, I thank you. I'm going to bury you. And your friend, here. I hope that will count for something."

The sound of his friend's horse came to him and he stood up. The Metis gave him one of the shovels and they began digging.

"I still don't know why you'd want to do a crazy thing like bury this buffalo. Lone Wolf—I can understand. Maybe we been up in them mountains too long, eh?" the Metis said, pausing to catch his breath.

"More digging and less talking, okay? My reasons are good enough for me."

Soon the hole was very large.

"Whew, you think it's big enough?" asked the Metis.

"I think so. Let's get the ropes."

They tied the ropes to the bison's body and then urged their horses to pull. The big bison sank to the bottom of the hole. They covered it and then laid Lone Wolf's body beside the white bison. They covered both bodies with the rest of the earth and tried to make the mound appear to be part of the natural rises in the ground so no one would bother with it.

The Metis wiped the sweat off his forehead with his shirt sleeve and then said with a grin, "Well, that was easier than I expected. Are you sure now that you don't want to bury the rest of them while you're at it?" He indicated the soldiers' bodies with a sweep of his arm.

The fair-skinned man looked thoughtful, then smiled and said, "Well, now that you mention it. . . ."

"Let's get going," the Metis cut in quickly. He mounted his horse, then looked at the other man. "You want to say some words, or something?"

"Already said them."

As they began riding off, the Metis said, "I don't know why we did that. But it makes me feel kind of good in a way."

* * *

Lone Wolf and I smiled. We watched both men ride off into the distance. And then we began our own journey to the Great Spirit world beyond. My spirit would return again in the future to walk with those who were gentle but strong. I would be seen by few, perhaps in visions, perhaps in dreams.

Beatrice Culleton is the author of *IN SEARCH OF APRIL RAINTREE*, first published in April 1983, and the revised edition, *APRIL RAINTREE*, published in December 1984.

Born on August 27, 1949, in St. Boniface, Manitoba, she was the youngest of four children. At the age of three, Beatrice became a ward of the Children's Aid Society of Winnipeg. She grew up in foster homes, away from her real family and her people, with the exception of several years when she lived in one foster home with one of her older sisters.

Because of her first book, Beatrice became involved with a group of Native people who were working towards a Native child care agency. She hopes to write a sequel to *APRIL RAINTREE*, sometime in the future, 'when the time is right'.

Order these fine books directly from Book Publishing Company:

Tofu Cookery .............................. $11.95
Tofu Quick and Easy ........................ 5.95
The Farm Vegetarian Cookbook ............... 7.95
Judy Brown's Guide
   to Natural Foods Cooking ................. 9.95
Kids Can Cook ............................. 8.95
Starting Over: Learning to Cook
   with Natural Foods ....................... 9.95
Vegetarian Cooking for Diabetics ............. 9.95
Murrieta Hot Springs Vegetarian Cookbook .... 9.95
George Bernard Shaw Vegetarian Cookbook .... 8.95
Ten Talents ................................ 16.95
Spiritual Midwifery ........................ 16.95
A Coop Method of Natural Birth Control ...... 5.95
The Fertility Question ...................... 5.95
No Immediate Danger ....................... 11.95
Shepherd's Purse:
   Organic Pest Control Handbook ............. 5.95
Song of Seven Herbs ....................... 9.95
Dreamfeather............................... 9.95
this season's people ........................ 5.95
A Basic Call to Consciousness ................ 7.95
How Can One Sell the Air? .................. 4.95
Spirit of the White Bison ................... 5.95

Please send $1 per book for postage and handling.

Mail your order to:
  Book Publishing Company
  PO Box 99
  Summertown, TN 38483